A JUST FOR A DAY BOOK

CATCHING THE WIND

JOANNE RYDER

ILLUSTRATED BY
MICHAEL ROTHMAN

MORROW JUNIOR BOOKS / NEW YORK

For Darl,
who has flown so far and soared high
with much joy and friendship

J.R.

In memory of my parents, Estelle and Martin Rothman

M.R.

Special thanks to Doug Ross, Director of Education for the Zoological Society of Manitoba, for his expert reading of the manuscripts of *Catching the Wind* and *White Bear, Ice Bear.*

Printed in the United States of America.
1 2 3 4 5 6 7 8 9 10
Library of Congress Cataloging-in-Publication Data
Ryder, Joanne.
Catching the wind / Joanne Ryder ; illustrations by Michael Rothman.
p. cm. — (A Just for a day book)
Summary: Transformed into a bird for a day, a child joins a flock
of wild geese in glorious flight.
ISBN 0-688-07170-8. ISBN 0-688-07171-6 (lib. bdg.)
[1. Geese—Fiction. 2. Birds—Fiction.] I. Rothman, Michael, ill.
II. Title. III. Series.
PZ7.R9752Cat 1989
[E]—dc19 88-23446 CIP AC

One fall morning
branches full of bright leaves
brush against your window:
shhhhh, shhhhh, shhhhh,
waking you gently.
You feel the wind
calling you softly,
changing you…

Till you reach up and the wild wind
catches you, carries you
out of your room
toward the wide bright sky.

The wind lifts you higher and higher
till it lets you go…
and you stretch your long neck
and beat your strong wings
till you catch the wind in them
and fly over the trees.

Your home, your street, your town
shrink far below you.
You are a wild bird soaring
between the earth and the clouds.
You are a wild bird,
wrapped in feathers.

Tiny black feathers
cover your long neck.
Tiny white feathers
make a patch on your chin.
Waterproof feathers cover your body,
long feathers, strong feathers
cover your wings.
And tucked underneath,
there is light soft down
to keep you warm
as you fly
through the cold windy sky.

Just ahead,
a dark *V* moves
under the white clouds.
Other wild birds are flying
in two long lines that meet.
Honk honk, honk honk.
Listen to them calling,
honking at the wind,
honking at the sky.

You answer in a new loud voice,
Here, I am…Here…
and listen till they call,
Come along, come along.

And you fly faster and faster,
beating your wings harder and harder
till you are the last one in line.
You are part of a flock, a flock of geese,
flying and honking across the sky.

You fly through the bright morning
over hills where cows look up
at you looking down at them.
You fly and fly
till you're hungry and tired,
and the goose at the head of the line
leads you from the sky
down and down and down.

Your webbed feet skim
the surface of cold water,
making ripples as you land
splashing and splashing.

You dip your smooth dark bill
into the shining water and drink.
The cool water slides
down your long, long throat.

You kick your webbed toes
open and closed, open and closed,
pushing yourself forward
across the small pond.

Then you climb up the slippery bank.
Your flat feet slap against the ground
and you sway through the grass.
With your sharp bill
you pluck the grass,
warm and sweet.

The afternoon sun warms you.
You curl your dark neck
and stroke your back,
brushing and oiling
your wind-tossed feathers
with your smooth bill.

Rested, the others call—
the fat goose,
the goose with the lame foot—
and then you, the new one,
join in, honking and honking.
And you spread your wings
and leap up high.

Two lines of geese
meet in the middle
and fly past the moon,
fly over gray cities
where gray smoke rises,
creeping, but not catching you.

And as they fly,
the other geese listen
to the wind singing to them,
Be warm.
Come, be warm.
But when you listen
you hear the wind
whispering,
Home.
Come home now.

And you,
the last goose in line,
fall behind, breaking the long *V*,
till the leader calls you,
Come, catch the wind.
Come and be warm.
Follow, follow us, now.
But you circle and turn,
honking one last time,
Goodbye…goodbye….

Back and back you fly,
till you soar above
a tiny faraway home
that calls to you, just to you.
Gliding down and down,
you pass the tall trees
with bright waving leaves
and slide through the open window,
where your own warm bed waits
to change you again.

So sleepy, you curl up
like a tiny bird in a nest,
snuggling under the sheets—
home for now.